My Beastie Book of

HarperCollinsPublishers

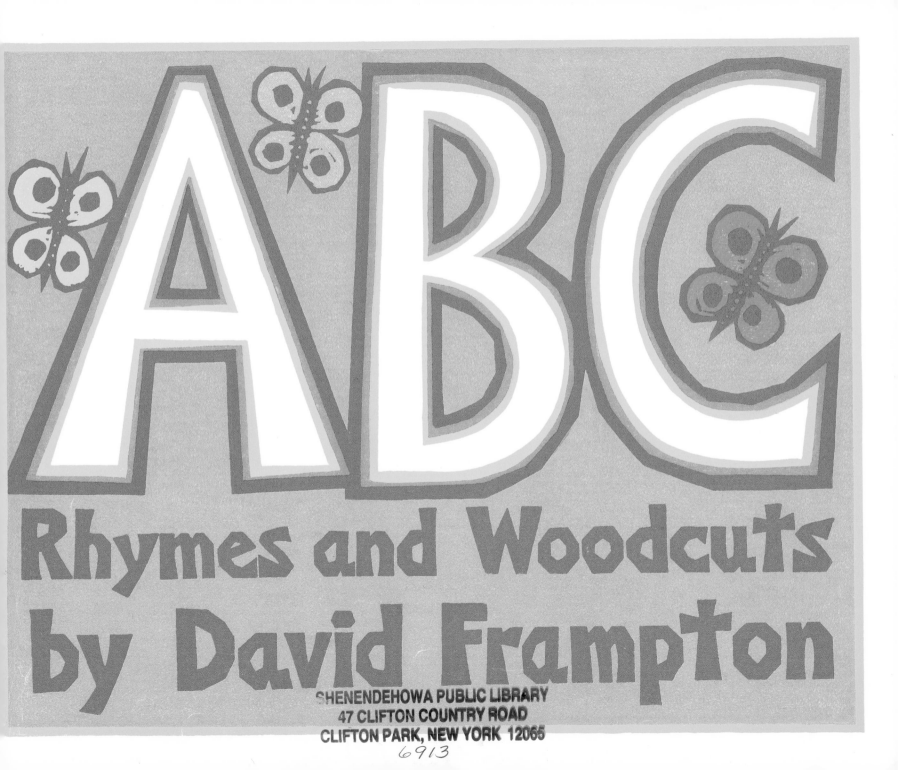

ABC

Rhymes and Woodcuts
by David Frampton

B is for butterflies up in the sky,
like silky bow ties all fluttering by.

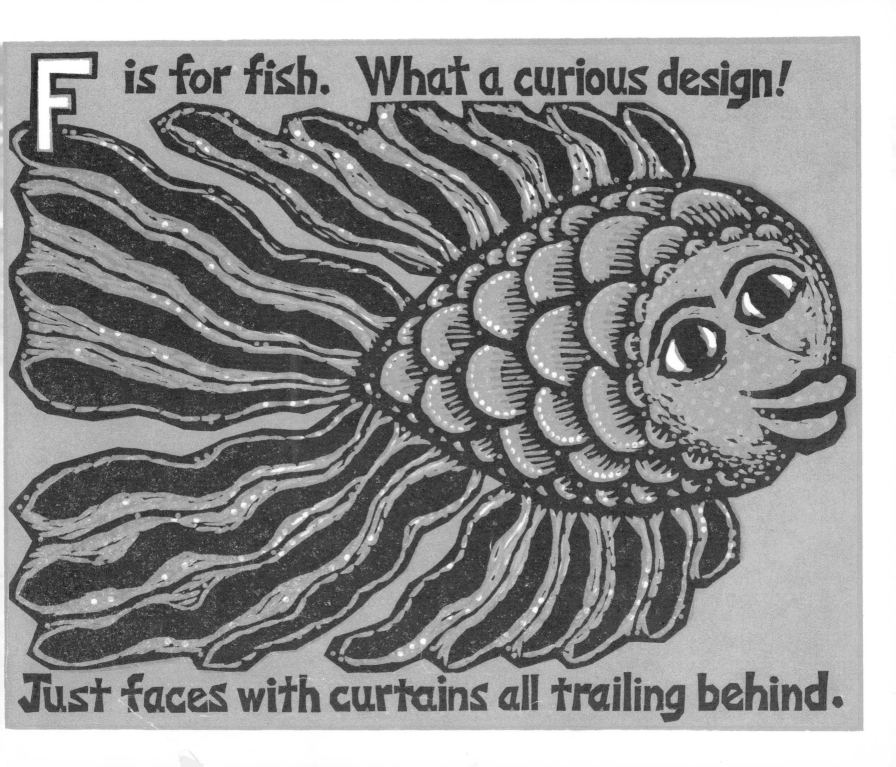

F is for fish. What a curious design!

Just faces with curtains all trailing behind.

G is for
grasshopper,
up down and up
over your sandwich
into your cup.

H is for hippo with mouth open wide.
You could easily fit a tricycle inside.
But then, it might be too yucky to ride.

I is for iguana.

I have one named Donna.
You can have one too,
unless you don't wanna.

P is for parrot.
I taught him a word.
He now can say "cheep".
Not bad for a bird!

R is for rhino as big as a jeep.

On her nose is a horn, but it won't go beep beep.

T is for tiger,
ferocious
and wild,

probably not a good pet for a child.

V is for vulture. They dine on decay.
A truly disgusting and smelly buffet.
But better than broccoli any old day!

X is for xog, an unusual pup.

I don't think you'll see one.
I just made him up.

For my children, Sarah and David, who have given me so much help on this book

My Beastie Book of ABC
Copyright © 2002 by David Frampton
Printed in the U.S.A. All rights reserved.
www.harperchildrens.com

Library of Congress Cataloging-in-Publication Data
Frampton, David.
  My beastie book of ABC : rhymes and woodcuts / by David Frampton.
     p.   cm.
  Summary: Illustrations and brief rhymes present an alphabet of
animals from alligator and hippo to parrot and zebra.
  ISBN 0-06-028824-8 (lib. bdg.) — ISBN 0-06-028823-X
  1. Animals—Juvenile poetry. 2. Children's poetry, American. 3. Alphabet
rhymes. [1. Animals—Poetry. 2. American poetry. 3. Alphabet.] I. Title.
PS3606.R36 M9 2002   2001039220
811'.54—dc21   CIP
                                                                      AC

1 2 3 4 5 6 7 8 9 10
❖
First Edition